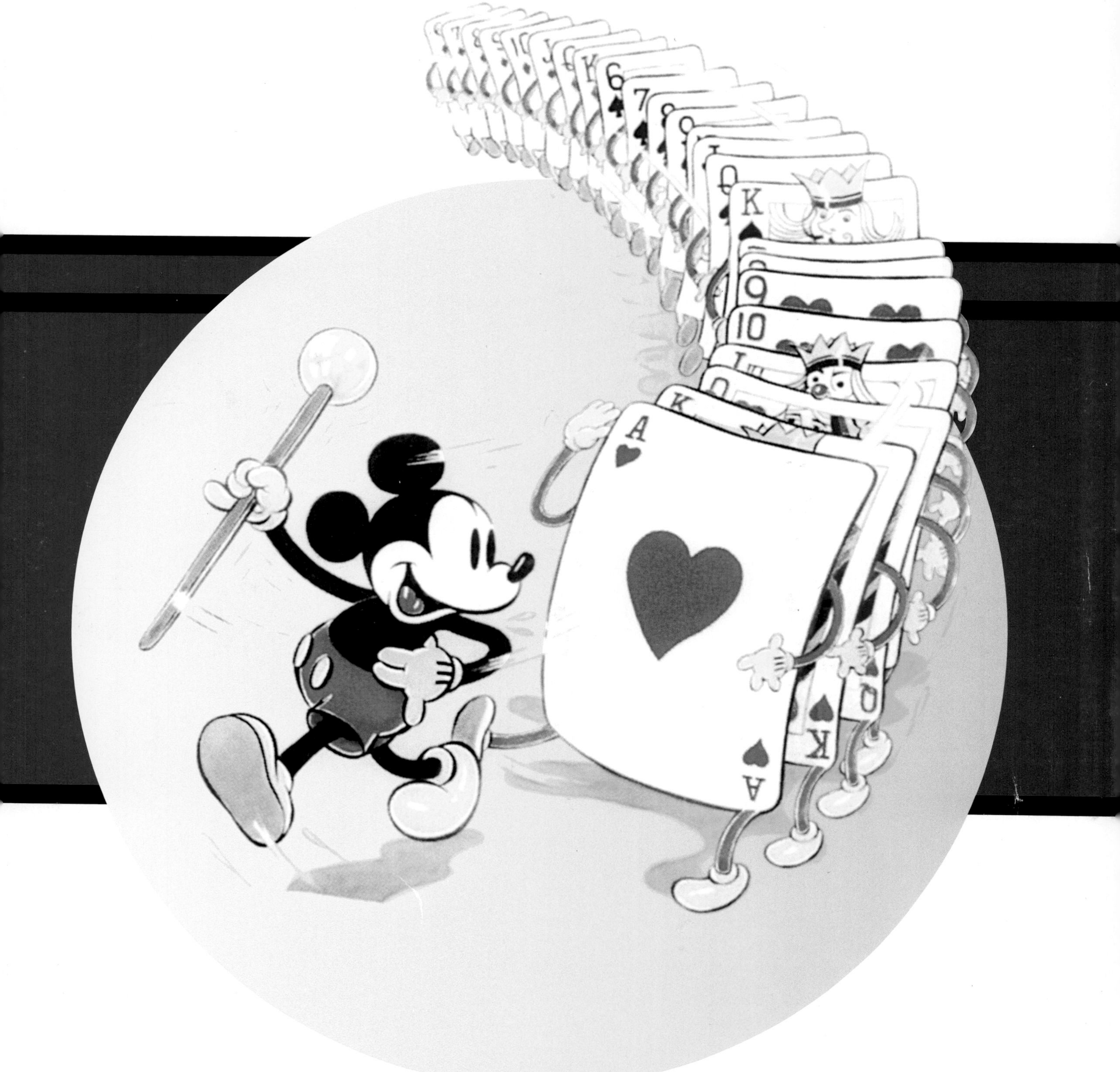

Walt Disney's MICKEY MOUSE TALES

Vintage tales from Disney's most popular animated short films

UNIVERSE

This edition published in the United States of America
in 2013 by Universe Publishing,
A Division of Rizzoli International Publications, Inc.
300 Park Avenue South
New York, NY 10010
www.rizzoliusa.com

2013 2014 2015 2016 / 10 9 8 7 6 5 4 3 2 1

Printed in China

ISBN: 978-0-7893-2473-3

Library of Congress Control Number: 2012950521

CONTENTS

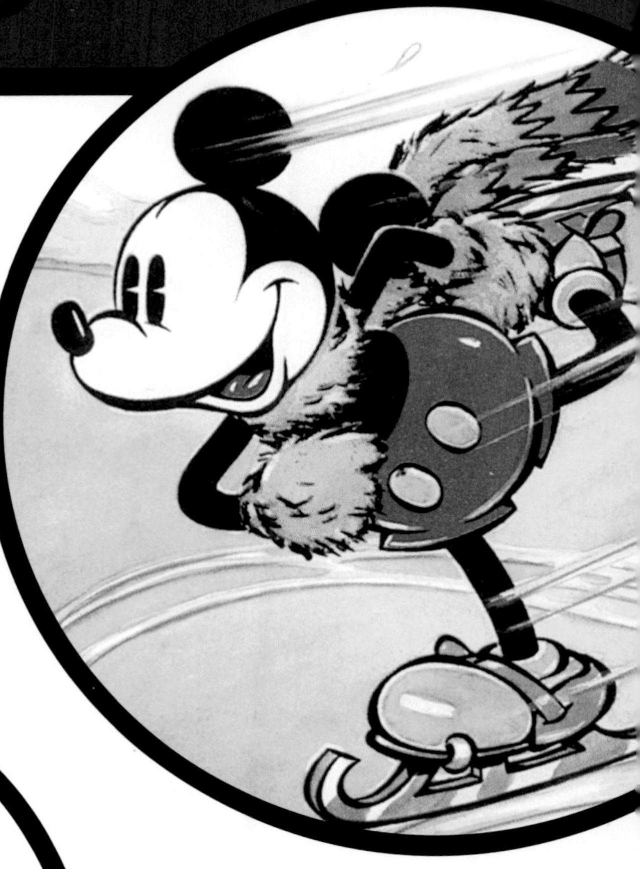

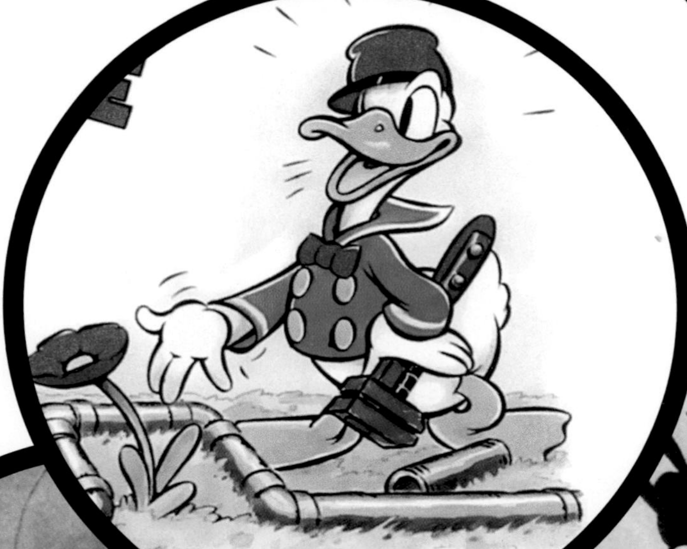

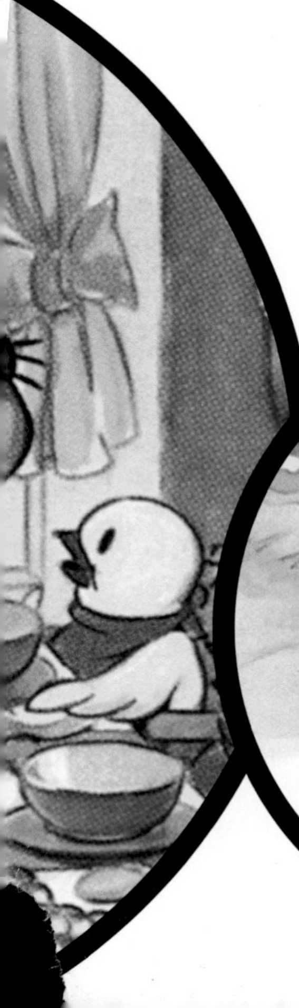

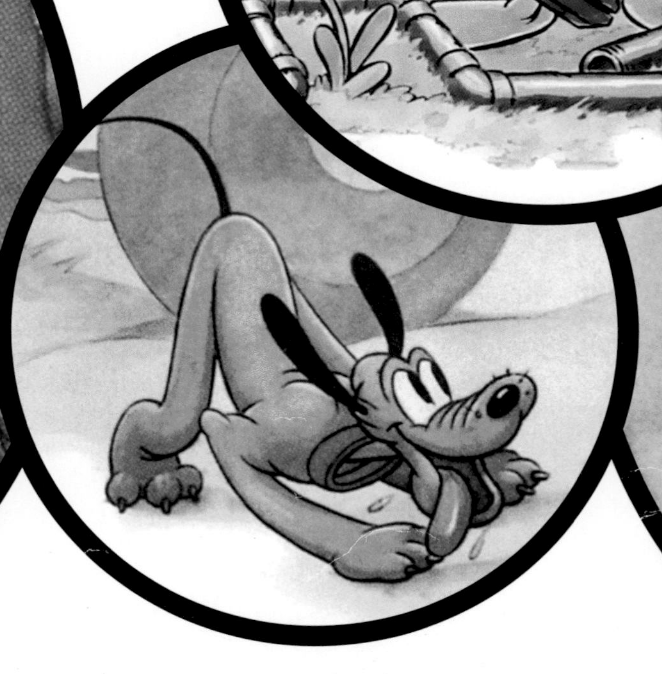

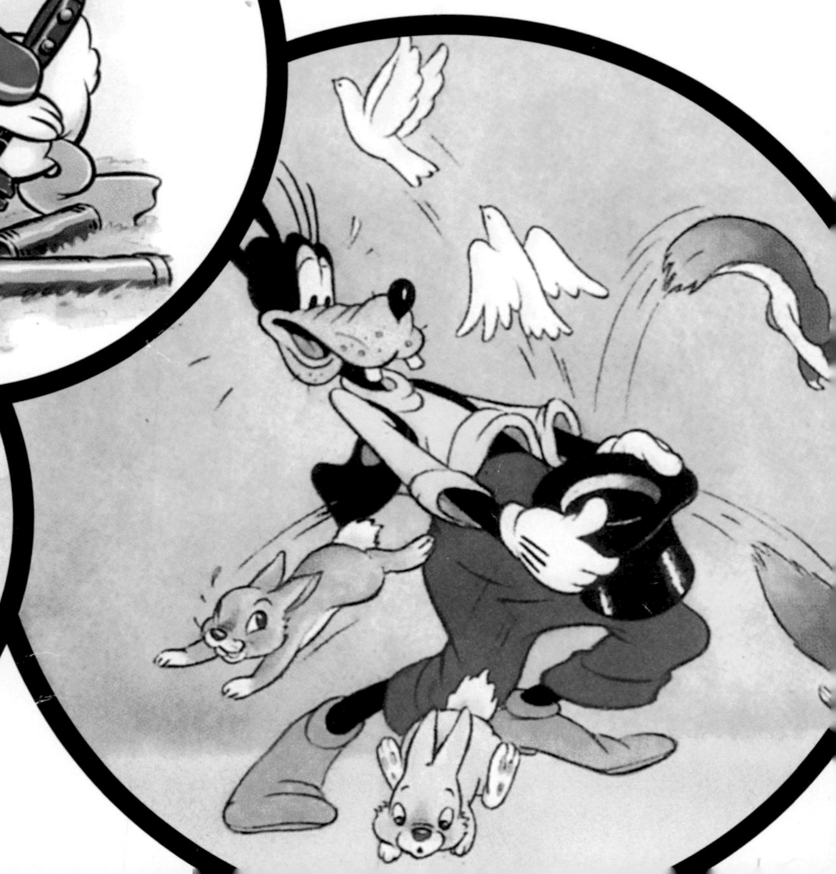

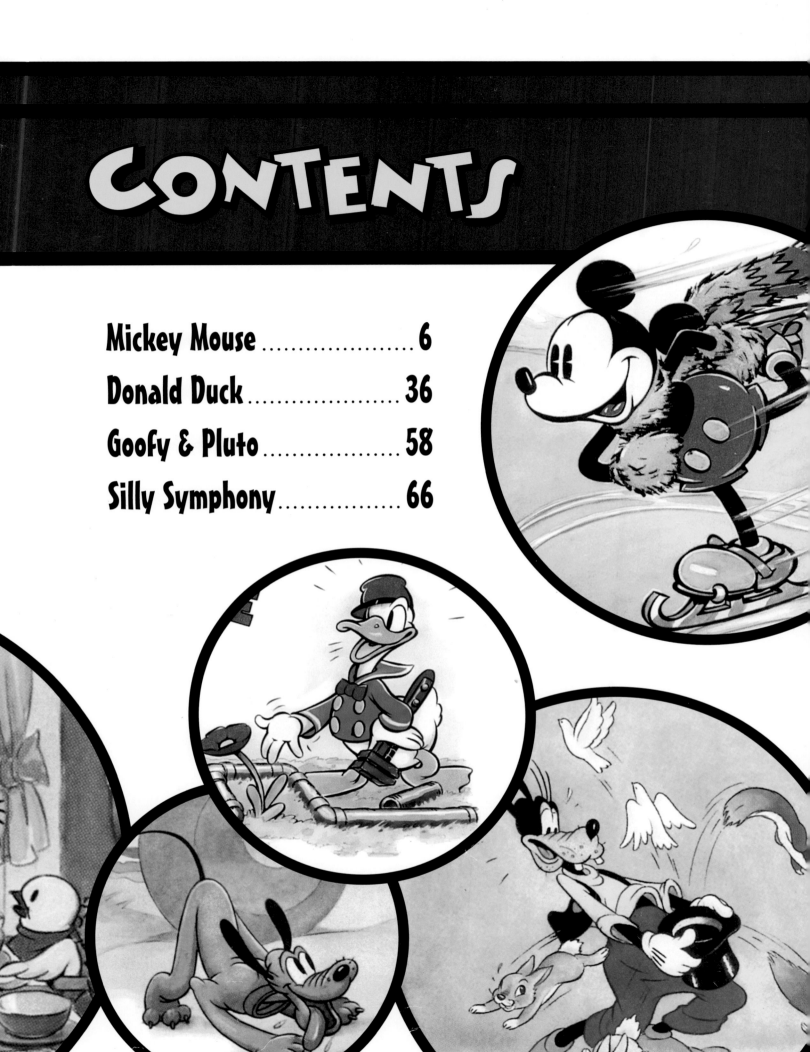

MICKEY MOUSE

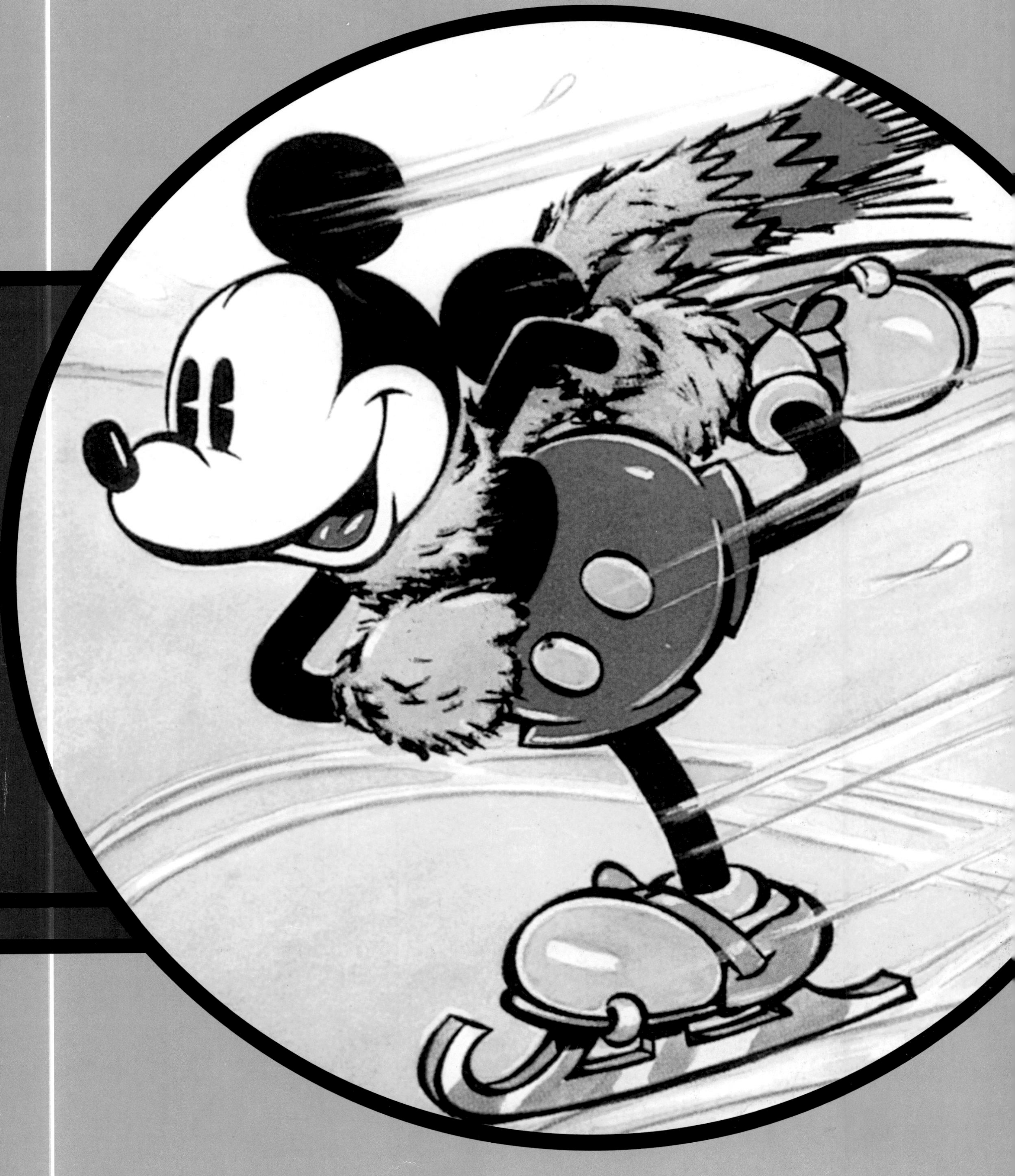

WALT DISNEY'S MICKEY MOUSE in 'The Band Concert'

Director Mickey lifts his hand
And starts to lead his barnyard band.
But Donald's clarinet cadenza
Sounds like a cat with influenza.

As a cornetist, Gideon Goat
Is quite a soloist of note.
But when poor Dippy's played four tunes,
His lips will look like unstewed prunes.

Long, long ago, Miss Clarabelle Cow
Played on the alto horn. But now?
Oh no! "A flute is best for me,
Because it's more high-toned," says she.

Biff! Boom! Clatter! BANG! That's Horace,
Pounding out an anvil chorus.
He makes an awful din and noise,
But it is just what he enjoys.

When Peter starts to play the tuba,
He can be heard from Maine to Cuba.
And yet the concert charms the crowd;
Not good—but very, VERY loud!

Mickey in his garden fell
    Asleep and dreamed one day
That all the bugs were big as he,
    And he as small as they.

The beetles were ferocious beasts,
    The worms were like huge snakes.
The dragon flies were giant size.
    Poor Mickey got the shakes.

'Mickey's Garden'
FROM THE
WALT DISNEY
MICKEY MOUSE

The snails were just like elephants
    That roared with mighty sound.
Intent on putting him to death,
    They chased him round and round.

The flies were armed with spray guns,
    And after him they flew.
"You've chased us long enough," they cried,
"So now we're chasing YOU!"

When he awoke, he said, "I used
    To hate to spray a fly;
But now I know that if they could,
    They'd do the same as I."

WALT DISNEY'S
MICKEY MOUSE

IN Mickey's Fire Brigade

A frightened call of: "Fire! Fire!"
A burst of smoke! The flames mount higher!
And rushing on the scene to aid
Comes Mickey Mouse's Fire Brigade.

For his part, Mickey quickly chose
To play the mammoth fire hose.
And then was Mickey's poor face red—
Because the hose played HIM instead!

Here we see the noble Goof,
Who loves to chop holes in the roof.
Of course no good is ever done
By this, but it's a lot of fun!

Inside the house, brave Donald spied
A woman. "Come with me!" he cried.
He rushed her out—and was he mad;
An old dress form was all he had!

When the smoke and flames have died,
Back the gallant fireman ride.
The fire was really a great success.
The house? Well, it burned down, I guess!

WALT DISNEY'S
MICKEY MOUSE
IN Mickey's Magic Hat

All sorts of things come popping from
    The magic hat of Mickey Mouse.
And does the crowd enjoy the act!
    His startling feats bring down the house!

Now Pluto takes a look and thinks,
    "This hat can't fool a pup like me!"
But out come rabbits, doves, and—Wow!
    The darn thing sprouts a Christmas tree!

"Attention, folks!" says Mickey now.
    "The hand is quicker than the eye!"
"Aw shucks! What hooey!" Donald jeers.
    "You couldn't fool a custard pie!"

The empty hat, then, Mickey shows.
    "Y'see—there's not a thing in there!"
He taps the hat, and from its crown
    Five little Donalds take the air!

The shock's too much for Donald's head:
    He's home with spots before his eyes.
And to himself he sadly thinks
    That Mickey must be pretty wise!

WALT DISNEY'S
MICKEY MOUSE
in "On Ice"

When winter season comes around,
Our Mickey gang can all be found
Upon the ice, while Mickey shows
Some fancy skating stunts he knows.

But Minnie, on the other hand
Is really very apt to land
'Most anywhere! And yet we feel
That she'll stand up at her next meal!

We sympathize with Pluto Pup—
He can't sit down, he can't stand up!
He slips and slithers, skids and slides,
And howls and yowls a bit besides.

See Dippy Dawg beside a hole:
He tells his pals that with his pole
He'll catch more fish than they can hold—
But all he catches is a cold!

Then Donald Duck falls in the lake
And freezes solid in a cake
Of ice! So all must sit about
A roaring fire and thaw him out!

"Say Donald, look at this old clock!"
Cried Mickey Mouse. "You know,
I'll bet you, if we cleaned it up,
That we could make it go!"

No sooner said than done! They popped
The clock into a tub,
And washed its hands and face, and gave
Its back a thorough scrub.

Then Donald dusted off the works,
As only Donald would,
And put them back—or, anyway,
He did the best he could.

"This cuckoo seems to lack detail,"
He said, "but I'll fix that!"
He did it with a broken plume
He'd found upon a hat.

And when they wound the clock, it went—
It went to pieces, quite!
"Well, anyhow," said Donald Duck,
"My cuckoo works all right!"

FROM A

WALT DISNEY
MICKEY MOUSE

▪ Mickey's Rival ▪

Mickey planned to have a quiet
   Picnic in the woods for two,
When on the scene burst Mortimer—
   A bragging bully, through and through.

While Minnie listened to his singing,
   Mickey wasn't miffed at all.
He knew that when a fellow's bragging,
   Pretty soon he takes a fall.

"I'm scared of nothing in the world,"
Mort said. "Why, I'm so rough and tough
I used to wrestle vicious bulls!"
—So Mickey simply called his bluff.

He found a bull and turned it loose!
Brave Mortimer let out a shriek!
And, as he ran, he howled with fear,
And beat the bull—into a creek.

More cake? You bet!" And Mickey grinned.
"He was so scared he almost died,
For, just like ev'ry hard-boiled egg,
He's yellow—when you get inside!"

WALT DISNEY'S
MICKEY MOUSE

Alpine Mickey

Mickey and Pluto and Donald Duck,
Determined and daring and full of pluck,
Went off to the mountains to try their luck,
With a yodel-hi-doodle-de-AY-hooooo!

Mickey went first, as the party's guide,
But Pluto got lazy and slowed their stride,
And Donald, the rascal, just went for the ride,
With an oodle-hi-lodle-de-AY-hooooo!

Donald demanded some edelweiss,
So Mickey eased both down over the ice,
But Pluto decided that wasn't so nice—
With an eedle-ho-laydle-de-AY-hooooo!

Mickey did all of the work for three,
while Pluto was tired as tired could be,
And Donald just yodeled and sang with glee,
With an aydle-hi-oodle-de-AY-hooooo!

When Mickey at last got the lazy pair
Clear up to the summit, he said, "I swear
That this is my last trip anywhere
With a couple of yodeling boob-boos!"

WALT DISNEY'S
MICKEY MOUSE
in Moving Day

If you are moving, take a tip
   From Mickey and his crew,
For they do things that even high-
   Class movers do not do!

For instance, if you have some fish,
   This portable aquarium
Is very handy, for you never
   Spill 'em while you carry 'em!

And if your barrels are too small,
   And china will not fit,
You'll find that you can force it in;
   Just ram it down a bit.

And if you can not get your clothes
   Into your trunk—all right!
Just take a pair of shears and trim
   Off everything in sight.

Then load the pile up on a cart,
   As only Mickey can.
And yet, somehow, we seem to feel
   We'd rather hire a van!

WALT DISNEY'S
MICKEY MOUSE
in Through The Mirror

Let's snore away to Mirror Land,
    Where Mickey has his dreams;
Where chairs and tables come to life,
    And nothing's what it seems.

In Mirror Land a footstool barks
    And wags its tassel tail;
A spinster armchair puffs her cheeks
    And says, "Outside, you male!"

18

So Mickey joins the Playing Cards—
 They always like parades.
With "Forward, march!" he leads the Hearts,
 Which irritates the Spades.

The King of Spades is envious.
 "Both swords will lick this clown!"
But Mickey wins—because the King
 Is one-half upside down!

Then Mickey hears a distant yelp—
 Of course it's Pluto Pup—
And Mickey reaches earth in time
 To find himself waked up!

WALT DISNEY'S MICKEY MOUSE

▪ Mickey's Circus ▪

Come one! Come all! Step right inside!
　　The band's about to play!
And Mickey Mouse's Three-Ring Show
　　Is getting under way!

Presenting: Duke Donaldo and
　　His troop of juggling seals.
He's very gay! (He knows that they
　　Like fish—not duck—for meals!)

A thrilling, gripping tightrope act
　　By Mickey. Hold your breath!
He whizzes on his one-wheeled bike,
　　Defying sudden death.

See Donald Duck! He walks the wire
　　And stands upon his head
Without a parasol or pole.
　　(He has balloons instead!)

These things and many more besides—
　　Gigantic! Huge! Immense!
Wild animals! A hundred acts!
　　Admission: Just three cents!

WALT DISNEY'S MICKEY MOUSE

PRESENTS

Mickey's Elephant

The mailman brought a grand new pet
 One day to Mickey Mouse—
He left a frisky elephant
 In front of Mickey's house.

When Pluto met him, he was just
 As pleased as he could be,
For Mickey said the elephant
 Could keep him company.

They set to work to build a place
 Where he could stay at night,
And Mickey measured fore and aft
 So it would fit just right.

He drew up fancy plans and made,
 To Pluto's great surprise,
A house shaped like an elephant,
 With space for trunk and eyes.

But when the place was ready for
 The roly-poly guest,
They found he'd squeezed in Pluto's house
 To take a little rest.

WALT DISNEY'S MICKEY MOUSE
Movie Makers

"LIGHTS! Camera! Action!" Donald cried.
But Pluto just lay down and sighed.
In fact he acted petrified—
    A temperamental star!

Then Mickey, candid cameraman,
Hit on a very clever plan.
So off Director Donald ran—
    He'd tempt his stubborn star!

He dangled under Pluto's nose
A kitten on a rubber hose,
Forgetting cats are natural foes
   To people like his star.

The action that ensued was hot.
Director Duck was on the spot—
The victim of his own bright plot
   To make a movie star!

The final scene was great indeed,
With Mickey grinding at full speed,
And Donald Duck, Director, treed—
   A most unlucky star!

WALT DISNEY'S MICKEY MOUSE
PRESENTS
Mickey's Amateurs

Mickey Mouse's Amateurs
    Put on a little show,
And Donald was the first to speak
    Upon the radio.

"Oh, winkle, crinkle, little star—"
    He started out all wrong,
And we were not surprised to hear
    That Donald got the gong.

When Clara Cluck began to sing,
    She cracked on every note;
She thought she would do very well,
    For she had sprayed her throat.

The Goof was introduced to play
    A horn that he had found;
But, though he blew with all his might,
    He couldn't make a sound.

He shook the horn, and Donald Duck
    A most determined bird,
Quacked, "'Twinkle, twinkle, little star—'
    Who says I won't be heard!"

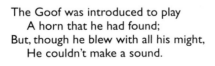

The baggagemaster, Donald Duck,
    Asks Mickey Mouse to see
An ostrich that is marked "Express"
    And "Handle Carefully."

Thet find a book which recommends
    Birdseed and fruit and berries.
But ostriches are not discussed—
    Just parrots and canaries.

They bring him birdseed, cake, and pie
    And such things till they're weak.
But at them all the ostrich just
    Turns up his nose—or beak!

They do not know, with ostriches,
    Much simpler food would do:
Some old tin cans, a yard of cloth,
    Perhaps a nice young shoe!

If Donald Duck had known these things,
    Which he did not, poor chap,
He might have kept his temper, and
    He would have kept his cap!

WALT DISNEY'S MICKEY MOUSE

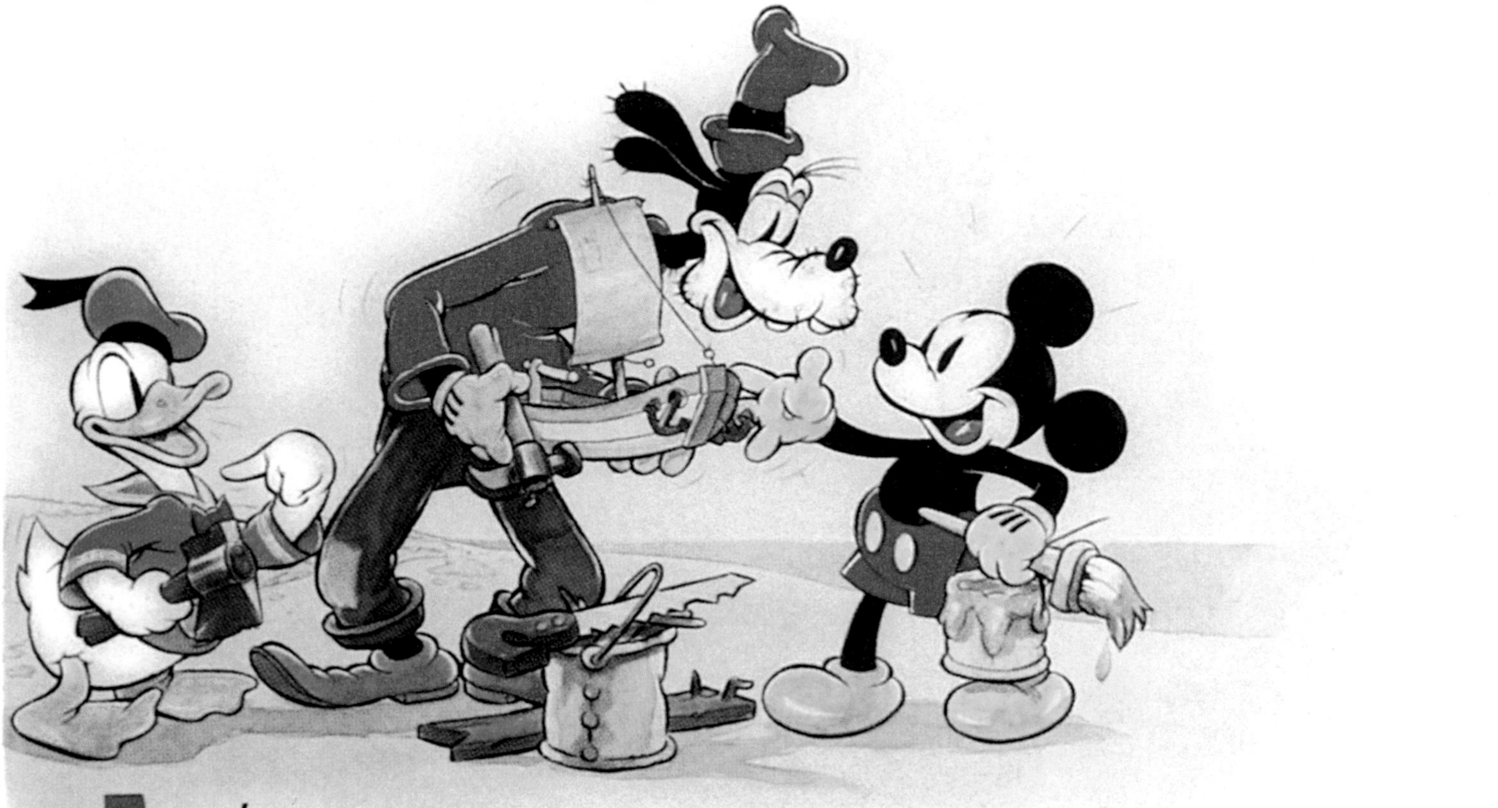

The Boat Builders

"Let's build a boat and be marines,"
Said Mickey to his pals one day.
"We'll sail the ocean blue in style—
But first we'll practice in the bay."

When it was finished, Donald got
As many anchors as he could.
He thought if one was nice to have,
Then ten would be ten times as good.

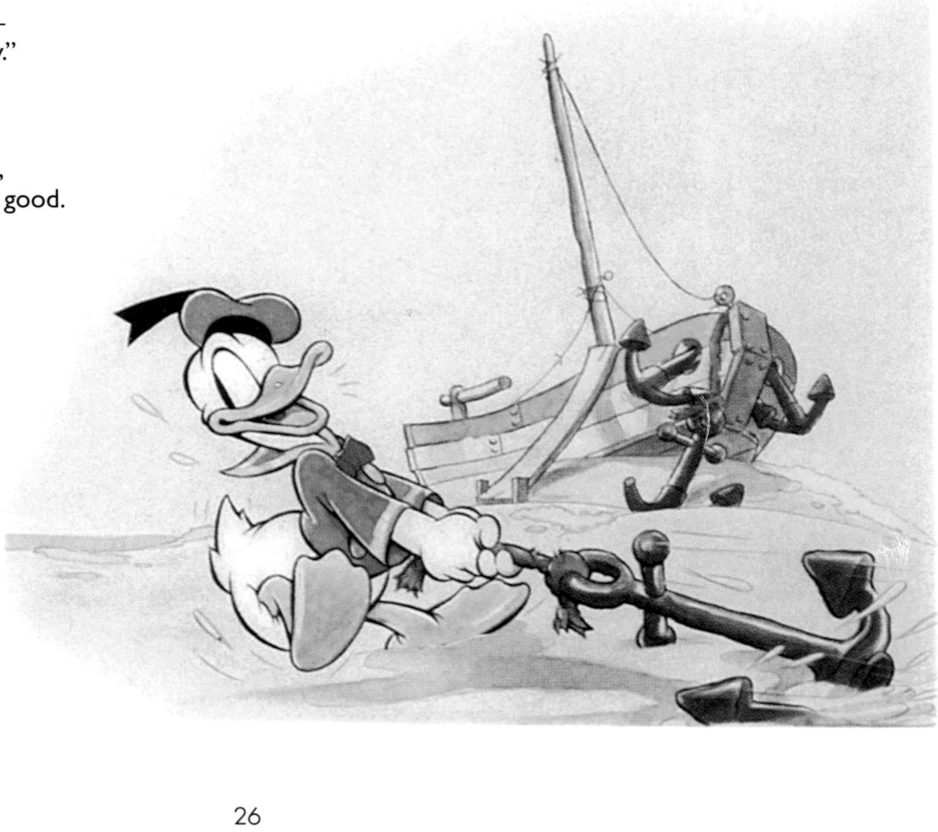

To make it safe the Goof drilled holes
  In stem and stern. The reason's plain—
In case the boat should spring a leak,
  The water'd run right out again.

They hoisted sail, blew up a breeze,
  And quickly down the ways they sped.
Behind them on the dock they left
  A sign—"We're out to launch!" it read.

The boat worked fine, except for just
  One little thing: it sank like lead.
Our friends were not marines at all,
  But soaking sub-marines instead.

WALT DISNEY'S MICKEY MOUSE

Mickey's Parrot

WHEN Mickey brought his new pet home,
    Poor Pol could only squawk.
So Mickey got his schoolbooks out
    To teach her how to talk.

Then Pluto came to get a drink—
    He was a bit abashed
To find that in his special dish
    A strange bird bathed and splashed.

But Pol had learned her lesson well,
    And, when she saw him there,
She called politely as could be,
    "Come in, the water's fair!"

Poor Pluto stayed to hear no more;
    He disappeared from sight.
A bird that talked! Was he awake?
    His hair stood up from fright!

But Polly, bound that they'd be friends,
    Had Mickey there to back her.
And soon she coaxed him out to play
    With "Pluto want a cracker?"

WALT DISNEY'S MICKEY MOUSE

Beach Picnic

IT WAS a bright and sunny day—
   A day to picnic at the shore;
So Mickey and the gang set out
   With bathing suits and food galore.

When Goof and Mickey went to swim,
   The faithful Pluto stood on guard.
But gulls and crabs could not resist
   A picnic in their own backyard.

The lunch was gone—but still it was
   A bright and sunny afternoon.
As Mickey floated blissfully,
   POP! Soon he'd lost his last balloon!

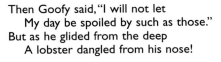

Then Goofy said, "I will not let
   My day be spoiled by such as those."
But as he glided from the deep
   A lobster dangled from his nose!

And then the rain began to fall;
   The lovely blue sky turned to gray.
Three damp and cold companions groaned,
   "It WAS a bright and sunny day!"

WALT DISNEY'S
MICKEY MOUSE
The Dog Show

"THE last Dog Show we had in town,"
 Said Mickey Mouse, "the pup
Who won it was a poodle dog—
 And, boy! as he slicked up!

"And so," he said, "I guess there's just
 One thing for us to do:
We'll do some slicking-up ourselves,
 And have a poodle, too."

30

No sooner said than done. And both
　　Were proud of what they'd found:
A thoroughbred unpedigreed
　　French Mongrel Poodle Hound!

To show him how he looked they put
　　A mirror on the floor.
Poor Pluto! He had never seen
　　A thing like that before!

A lion? Tiger? Bear? Or dog?
　　Or what? He didn't know.
And all that he could think of was
　　One word—and that was: GO!

WALT DISNEY'S
MICKEY MOUSE
" SOCIETY DOG SHOW "

POOR Pluto had no pedigree
With which to face society,
But Mickey loved him tenderly
And put him in the show.

Since Mickey thought it only fair
To give his pet the finest care,
He made him up and groomed his hair
So he might win the show.

But Pomeranians and Chows
Rolled languid eyes and lifted brows
And asked in low, refined bowwows
How *he* got in the show.

Alas, alack! Disaster came
Before the judge called Pluto's name:
The place was filled with smoke and flame;
The dogs all left the show!

But one small pup of half-pint size
Was caught when smoke got in his eyes.
And Pluto, hero, got grand prize
As champion of the show!

WALT DISNEY'S MICKEY MOUSE
The Pointer

WHEN Mickey read about Big Game,
 He thought it would be fun
To raise his brand-new gun and aim,
 And see his victims run.

So off they went upon a trek,
 For Pluto was to point;
And Pluto pointed till his neck
 Was nearly out of joint.

At last! The scent of some wild beast!
 Fierce Pluto forged ahead.
He thought 'twould be a bear, at least,
 Till he saw *this* instead.

A tiny squirrel blinked its eyes
 As if to plead, "Oh, why?"
And Pluto, feeling half his size,
 Was 'shamed enough to die.

So Mickey threw away his gun
 To play a nicer game.
He said, "My hunting days are done";
 And Pluto felt the same.

Brave Little Tailor

"**B**RING on your giant!" Mickey bragged.
   "With trusty shears and thread
I'll capture him; then, Minnie mine,
   Perhaps we two shall wed!"

The King heard Mickey's reckless boast
   And took him at his word.
As Giant Killer Number One
   The tailor felt absurd.

The giant was a fearsome thing;
   Like thunder was his sneeze.
But little Mickey tripped him on
   A rope between two trees!

The giant fell and shook the earth.
   Then Tailor Mickey sped
To get the weapons of his trade—
   His scissors and his thread.

He sewed the monster up so tight
   He couldn't get away.
And Princess Minnie was so thrilled
   That they were wed that day!

WALT DISNEY'S
MICKEY MOUSE

MR. MOUSE TAKES A TRIP

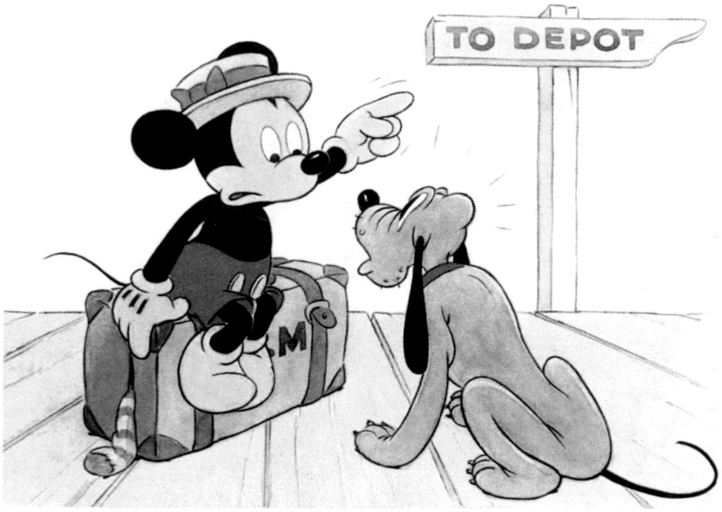
TO DEPOT
M.M

SAID Mickey, "Come, let's see the world!"
He packed his little grip,
And he and Pluto started off
To take a little trip.

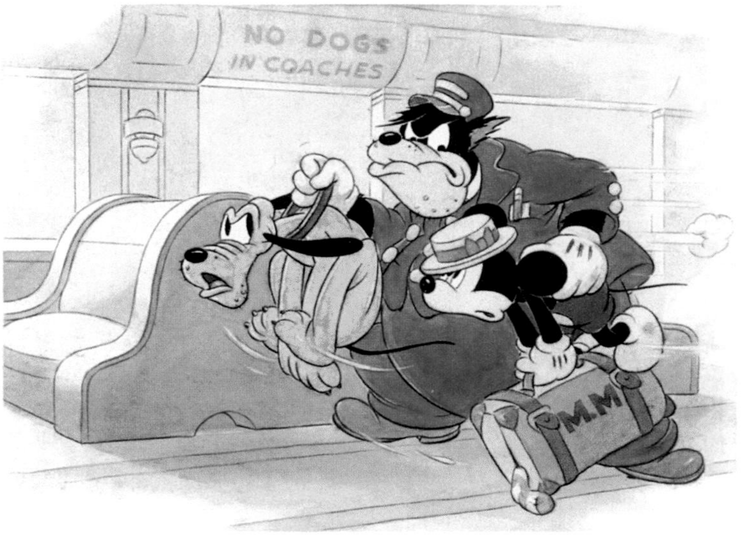
NO DOGS
IN COACHES
M.M

But when Conductor Pete stalked through,
All Mickey's pleas were vain.
The rules were strict. "No dogs!" he roared,
And put them off the train.

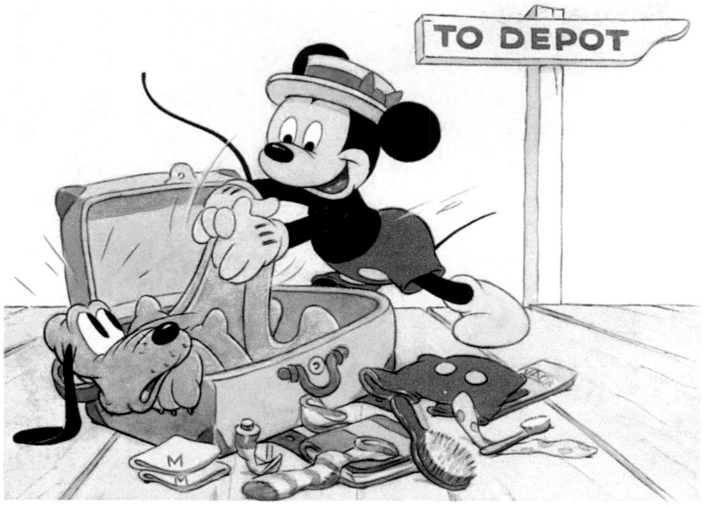
TO DEPOT

So Mickey, not discouraged, said,
"We'll fool that guy, I'll bet."
And once again, he packed his bag—
In went his awkward pet!

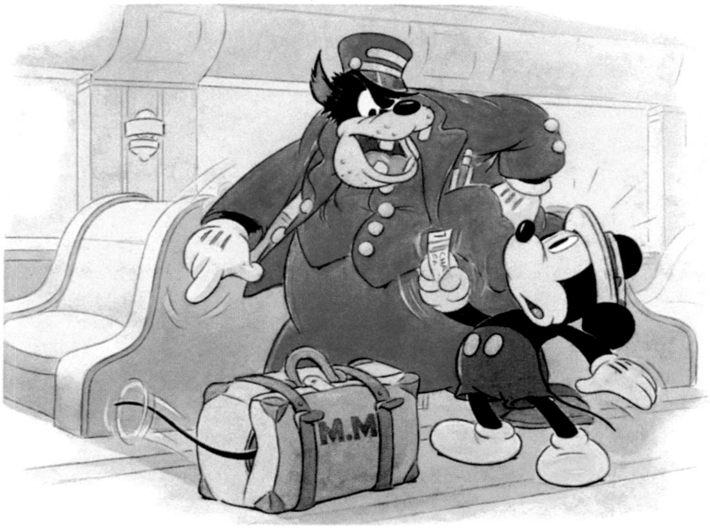
M.M

But next time Pete came through the train,
His roars made Mickey quail.
"No dog, you say?" he pointed out.
"Well, whereby hangs that *tail?*"

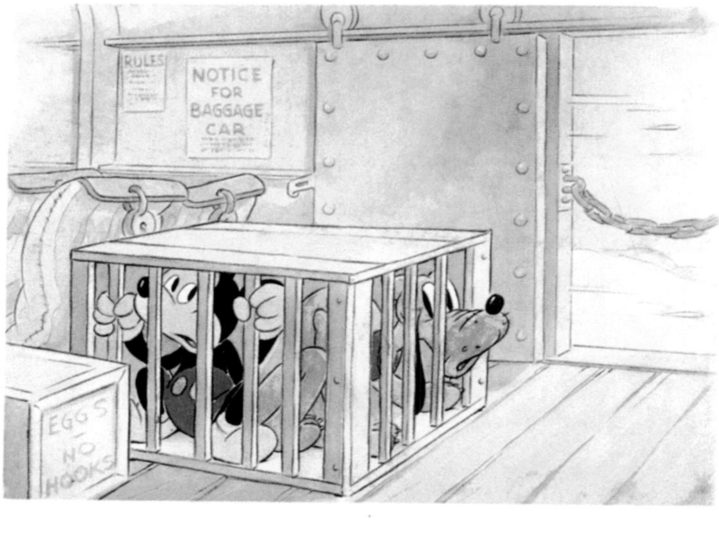
RULES
NOTICE
FOR
BAGGAGE
CAR
EGGS
NO
HOOKS

At last the weary trav'lers in
The baggage car lay curled.
Said Mickey, "Pluto, now we know
How *not* to see the world!"

THE LITTLE WHIRLWIND

"I'M GLAD that's done," said Mickey Mouse,
"For it's a job worth while.
At last those frisky autumn leaves
Are raked into a pile!"

Oho! What's this—a whirlwind? "Hey!"
Hear Mickey's frantic cry.
"Why don't you stay where you belong?
Get back into the sky!"

"Go 'way!" he yells. "I'll mow you down!
And that's not all I'll do.
If you will just hold still a bit,
I'll break you right in two!"

Poor Mickey speaks the words too soon;
The whirlwind will not stop.
Instead, it grabs him, rake and all
And spins him like a top!

"It's gone, but see what's left behind,"
Sighs Mickey. "I perceive
I'm just so irresistible
The leaves refused to leave!"

WALT DISNEY'S MICKEY MOUSE
"CANINE CADDY"

"Let's play a game of golf today.
I'll show you how it's done,"
Said Mickey. "I'll tee off right here
And make this hole in one."

He drives too long; he putts too short;
The ball sails east and west.
It simply won't roll in the cup,
And Mickey is distressed!

Determined Mickey tries again.
Another swing—and miss!
The weary caddy thinks that he
Can't stand much more of this!

Poor Mickey wonders what to do;
But Pluto thinks 'twould seem
A good idea to make make one hole
As big as all eighteen.

So be like Mickey—don't give up
In any work or play,
Because some unexpected help
Will often save the day.

WALT DISNEY'S MICKEY MOUSE
"MICKEY'S BIRTHDAY PARTY"

Surprise for Mickey Mouse today!
His friends all congregate
To wish him Happy Birthday and
To help him celebrate.

Their bulky gift turns out to be
An organ; so of course
He plays "Hail, hail, the gang's all here."
They sing until they're hoarse.

And Goofy, in the time between,
Stirred up the birthday cake;
This most magnificent affair
Was difficult to bake.

He told his pal to blow and wish;
But just as Mickey blows,
Poor Goofy's foot slips on a rug,
And down the whole thing goes.

"My wish," said Mickey woefully,
"It never could come true.
I should have known I couldn't have
My cake and eat it, too!"

DONALD DUCK